Hot Rod Hamster
and the Haunted Halloween Party!

By Cynthia Lord

Cover illustration by Derek Anderson

Interior illustrations by Greg Paprocki

Scholastic Press • New York

To Emily. — C. L.

For my grandparents, Walter and Margaret Schwab,
who always had treats! — D. A.

Text copyright © 2015 by Cynthia Lord
Illustrations copyright © 2015 by Derek Anderson
All rights reserved. Published by Scholastic Press, an imprint of Scholastic Inc., *Publishers since 1920.*
SCHOLASTIC, SCHOLASTIC PRESS, and associated logos are trademarks and/or registered trademarks of Scholastic Inc.

LIBRARY OF CONGRESS CATALOGING-IN-PUBLICATION DATA AVAILABLE

ISBN 978-0-545-81529-1

10 9 8 7 6 5 4 3 2 1   15 16 17 18 19

Printed in Malaysia   108
First edition, August 2015

The display type was set in Ziggy ITC and Coop Black.
The text was set in Cochin Medium and Gill Sans Bold.
The interior art was created digitally by Greg Paprocki.
Art direction and book design by Marijka Kostiw

It was Halloween. Hot Rod Hamster hurried off to find his friend Dog. He was on the run to show Dog something fun.

Dog, look what came in the mail!
It's a Halloween party! There will be prizes, games, food, and fun! Let's go!
WHAT?
Halloween Party
WHEN?
October 31. From 5 to 8 p.m.
WHERE?
The town square
WHO?
YOU! Bring your friends, too.
Prizes for the best and the spookiest costumes!
FUN! GAMES! FRIGHTFULLY GOOD FOOD!

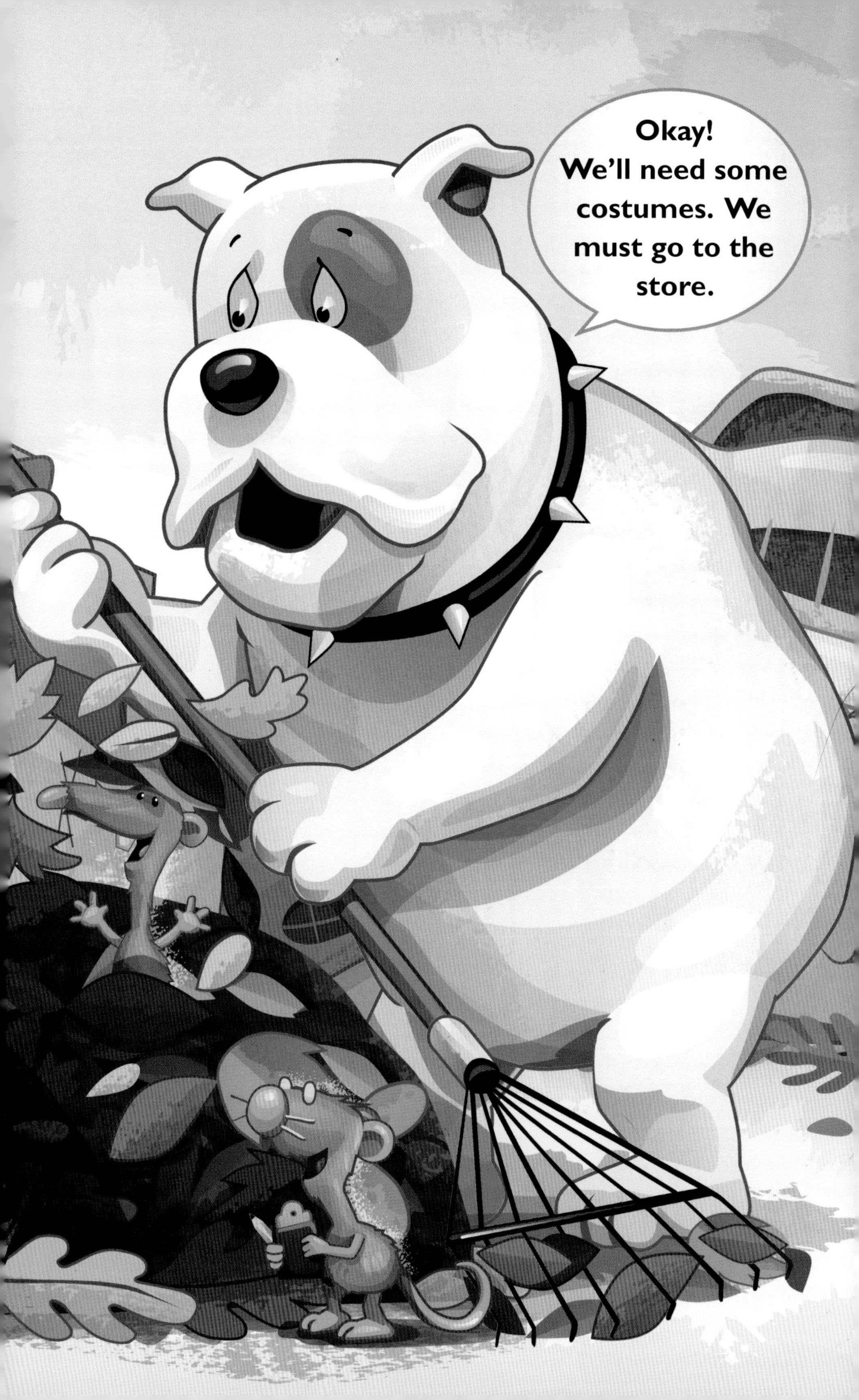
Okay!
We'll need some costumes. We must go to the store.

Ghost fun. Clown fun.
Star fun. Crown fun.

Which would *you* choose?

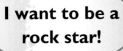

Shake it.

Drum it.

Blow it.

Strum it.

Which would *you* choose?

I'm ready to rock and roll! Maybe we'll win the prize for best costume!

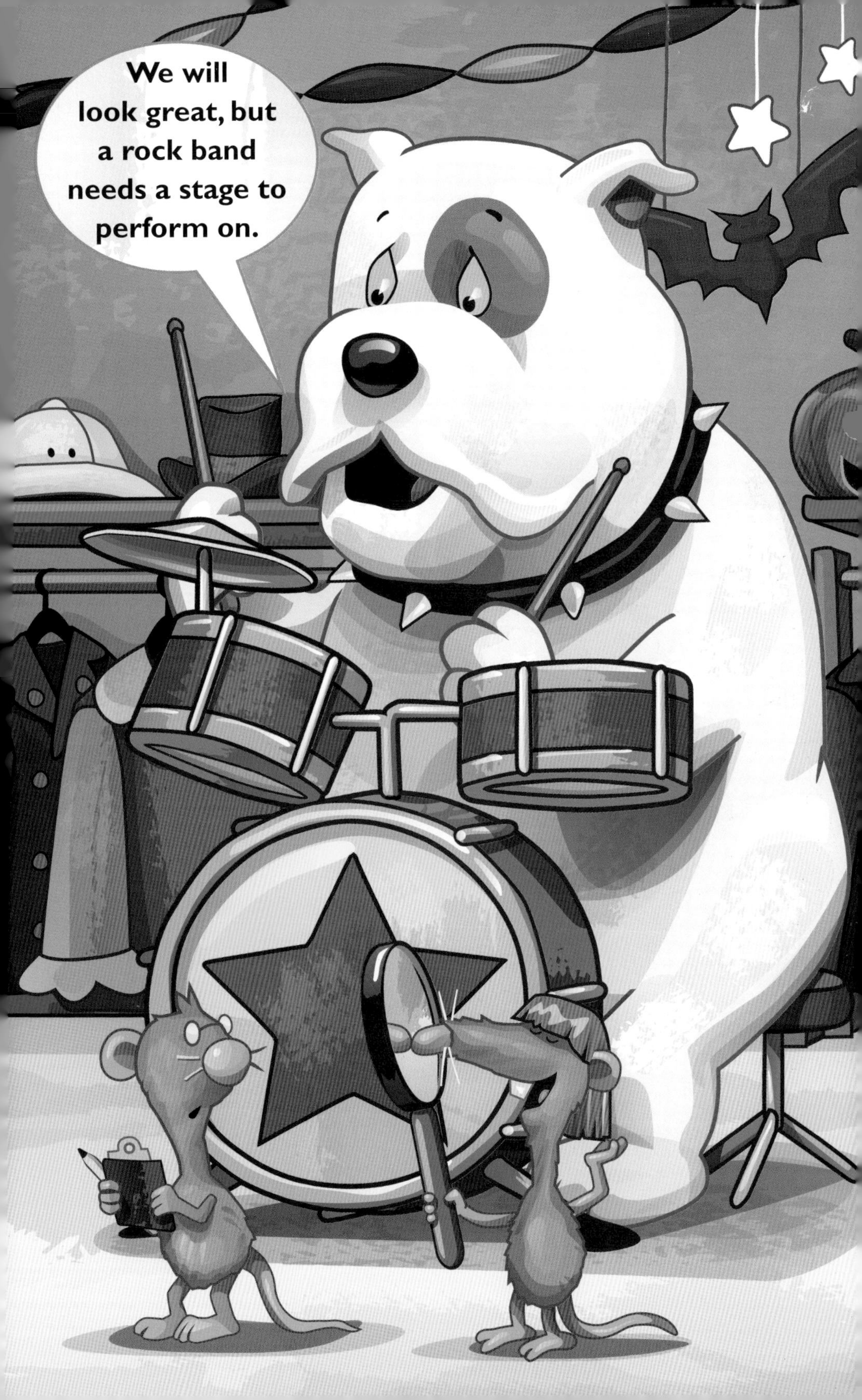
We will look great, but a rock band needs a stage to perform on.

Dog builds a stage.
Hamster makes it glow.
Mice add some glitz.
Almost time to go!

HALLOWEEN
STUFF

Now we need a spooky song to sing. *Halloween is fun and spooky, too!* What rhymes with "too"?

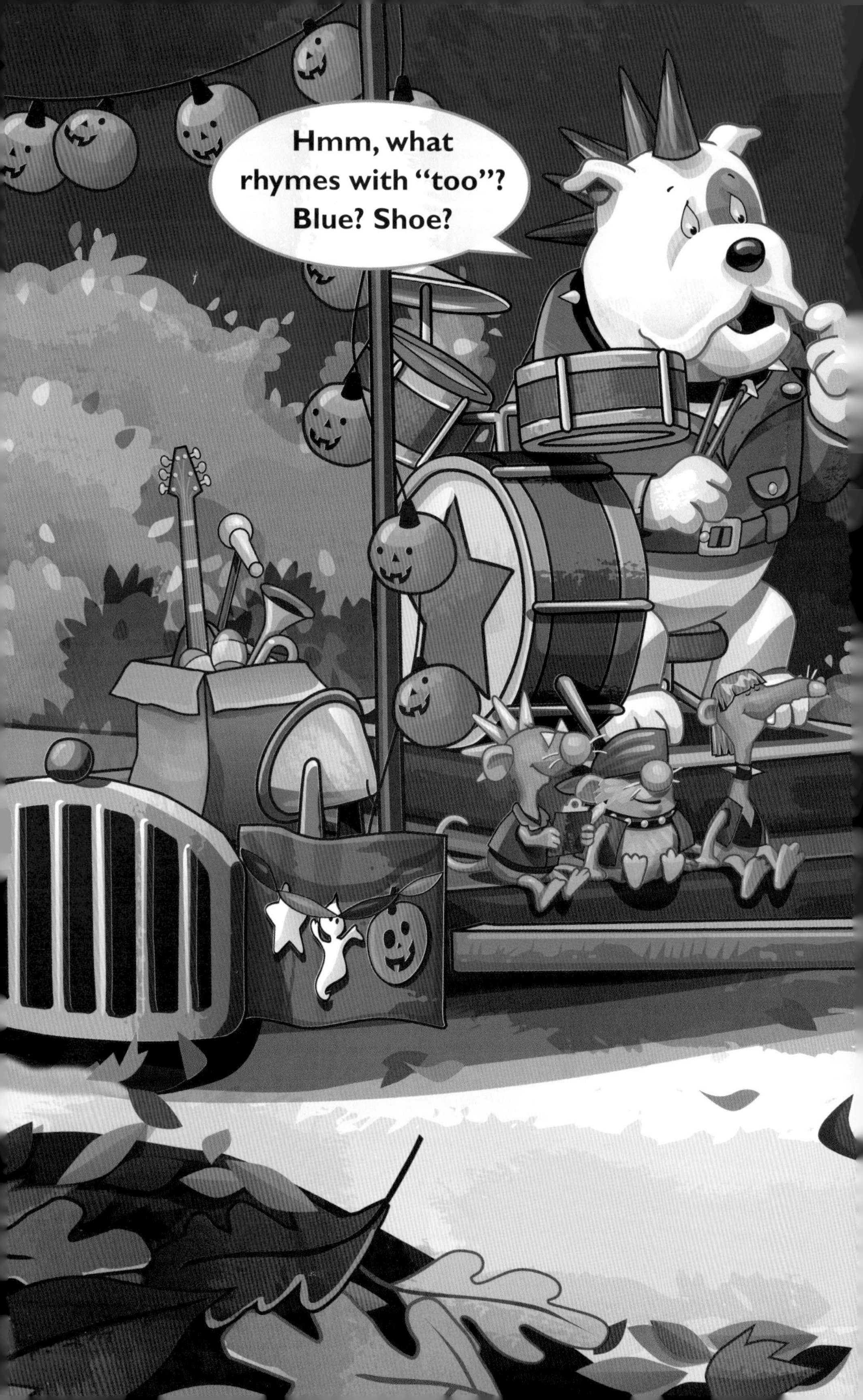
Hmm, what rhymes with "too"? Blue? Shoe?

Dog tries to help Hamster with his song.
Mice dream of fun, but—oh no!
Something's wrong.

I'm sorry. The hot rod has broken down. I could fix it if I had some tools.
It's almost time for the party. Let's ask for help at this house.

Dog isn't sure, but Hamster steps inside . . .

Mice stop and gasp. Their eyes open wide.

Do you have some tools we could borrow? Our car broke down and we're late for a party.

Ooooh, a party?
I love parties!
Does the party have treats? And music?
If we loan you the tools, can we come to the party, too?
I have a great idea!

Carve time?

Sweet time?

Drink time?

Meet time?

Which would *you* choose?

Dog carves pumpkins.
Hamster tastes the brew.

Ghosts float around
and practice saying "Boo!"

Boo!

It's time for the
costume judging!
Everyone get
ready!

Dog taps the beat.
Hamster counts a few.

Here we go!
One, two,
three, four!

Mice take their spots,
backup singers, too.

Dog plays the drums.
Hamster sings his song.
Mice shake and dance.
The ghosts howl along.

Hot Rod Hamster and His Howl-Agains!
Thank you! HAPPY HALLOWEEN, EVERYONE!